HEALTH & FITNESS

DRINKING, SMOKING, AND OTHER DRUGS

Emma Haughton

RSVP

RAINTREE
STECK-VAUGHN
P U B L I S H E R S
A Steck-Vaughn Company

Austin, Texas

www.steck-vaughn.com

ADOLESCENCE

DIET AND NUTRITION

DRINKING, SMOKING, AND DRUGS

EXERCISE

Published by Raintree Steck-Vaughn Publishers,
an imprint of Steck-Vaughn Company

Library of Congress Cataloging-in-Publication Data
Haughton, Emma.
Drinking, smoking, and other drugs / Emma Haughton.
  p. cm.—(Health & fitness)
  Includes bibliographical references and index.
  Summary: Explains the nature of drugs, both legal and illegal,
 how they can affect the body, and how they can help or harm users.
  ISBN 0-7398-1345-5
  1. Drugs—Juvenile literature.
  2. Substance abuse—Juvenile literature.
  [1. Drugs. 2. Drug abuse.]
  I. Title. II. Series.
  RM301.17.H38 2000
  615'.7—dc21   99-36216

Printed in Italy. Bound in the United States.
1 2 3 4 5 6 7 8 9 0 04 03 02 01 00

Picture acknowledgments:
Digital Stock *cover band* bottom; Digital Vision 42; Image Bank 4 (Rod Westwood), 10 (David de Lossy), 11 (David de Lossy), 20 (Gabriel Covian), 22 (Bokelberg), 24 (Nicholas Russell), 28 (Color Day), 31 top (Color Day), 32 (Steve McAlister), 40 (Barros & Barros); Science Photo Library 16 (Dr. E. Walker), 18 (Damien Lovegrove), 25 bottom (A. Glauberman), 29 (Jim Selby), 35 (Wesley Bocxe), 37 (Cordelia Molloy), 38 (BSIP Laurent), 39 (Tek Image), 41 (Cordelia Molloy), 43 (Will & Deni McIntyre); Stock Market *front cover* main image, 1, 5 (Robert Cerri), 9, 13, 19, 23, 26, 27 (Roy McMahon), 45; Tony Stone Images *cover band* middle (Andy Sacks), 6 (David Harry Stewart), 7 (Steve Taylor), 8 (Jean-Marc Truchet), 12 (Peter Dokus), 14 (Chad Slattery), 17 (Douet/TSI Imaging), 21 (Tim Hazael), 31 bottom (Simon Norfolk), 33 (Demetrio Carrasco), 34 (David Young Wolff), 36 (Zigy Kaluzny), 44 (Mark Harwood); The artwork on the cover and on pages 15 and 25 is by Michael Posen.

CONTENTS

WHAT IS A DRUG?

Cigarettes (containing nicotine) and coffee (containing caffeine) are widely used across the world.

A drug is a substance or chemical that affects the way your body or your mind works. Some drugs are artificially made. Others come from plants, minerals, and even animals.

DRUGS IN HISTORY

Human beings have used drugs for thousands of years as medicines, to change the way they experience the world, or simply for pleasure. Over 10,000 years ago, American Indians used mescal beans as a stimulant. The Chinese have had herbal medicines for more than 5,000 years.

HOW PEOPLE TAKE DRUGS

You can take drugs in various ways. When you drink or swallow them, they enter the bloodstream via the stomach. Some are smoked or inhaled via the lungs. Others are administered by injection. With patches, suppositories, or creams, the active ingredients are absorbed through the skin.

WHAT ARE DRUGS?

When someone mentions drugs, we often think of illegal substances like heroin, cocaine, or cannabis, but there are many other kinds of drugs. Chances are, you have taken several yourself. Most people have had aspirin or acetaminophen for a headache, or antibiotics for an infection. If you drink coffee, tea, cola, or even eat chocolate, you will have consumed a stimulant drug called caffeine. Two of the most common drugs taken by adults are alcohol and tobacco.

Some drugs derive from things designed for other purposes. Solvents, for instance, used widely in glues and other household products, can have powerful effects when inhaled.

WHERE DO DRUGS COME FROM?

New drugs are discovered every day. Medicines are often made up from chemicals in a laboratory, but many are extracted from plants. One reason people are so concerned about destruction of the Amazon rain forest is that so many of our useful drugs have come from plants discovered there.

When it was first manufactured, Coca-Cola contained the drug cocaine, which is now illegal. Coca-Cola still contains the stimulant drug caffeine, which is legal. Caffeine is also found in coffee and tea.

WHERE DRUGS COME FROM

NAME	WHAT IS IT?	WHERE DOES IT COME FROM?
Aspirin	Painkiller	Bark of the willow tree
Caffeine	Stimulant	Coffee beans, cocoa, and tea leaves
Cannabis (marijuana)	Recreational drug	*Cannabis sativa* plant
Digitalis	Heart drug	Foxglove
Taxol	Anti-cancer drug	Yew tree
Tobacco	Recreational drug	*Nicotiana tabacum* plant

LEGAL AND ILLEGAL DRUGS

Drugs are strong substances. They can have powerful effects on our bodies and our minds. For that reason, many countries and cultures have forbidden some drugs, either by religion or law. In most Western countries, drugs like heroin, cocaine, speed, ecstasy, and cannabis are illegal to sell and to buy. In Muslim countries like Saudi Arabia, alcohol is illegal. Many illegal drugs have been so for only a relatively short time. Until earlier this century, cocaine was a main ingredient in Coca-Cola. In Great Britain, opium, a relative of heroin, was freely available until the late eighteenth century. It was only when doctors became aware of their dangers and addictiveness that governments banned these drugs.

Alcohol and cigarettes are widely regarded as "social" drugs, meaning that groups of people can enjoy them together. People who become dependent on alcohol or cigarettes often find it hard to socialize without a drink or cigarette.

THE STRENGTH OF DRUGS

Whether a drug is legal or illegal doesn't necessarily relate to how powerful or dangerous it is. Too much alcohol or tobacco, for instance, can shorten your life considerably. Alcohol can also make you a danger to other people, especially if you drink and drive. Some people say this means we should legalize drugs like cannabis. They argue that it doesn't make sense to ban some drugs, while other powerful and dangerous ones are legal.

IS IT LEGAL (UNITED STATES AND GREAT BRITAIN)?

Drug	Is it legal?	Constraints
Alcohol	Yes	Not legal for children
Amphetamines (e.g. speed)	Yes	As a prescribed appetite suppressant
Cannabis	No	Some U.S. states allow possession of small amounts
Cocaine	No	
Ecstasy	No	
Hallucinogenic drugs (e.g. LSD)	No	
Heroin	No	
Morphine	Yes	Only as a prescribed painkiller
Sleeping pills (e.g. barbiturates)	Yes	Only by prescription
Tobacco	Yes	Not legal for children
Tranquilizers (e.g. Temazepam)	Yes	Only by prescription

CONTROL OF DRUGS

Medicinal drugs are controlled in different ways. Some, like many painkillers, can be bought freely in drugstores and supermarkets. Most, however, are available only by prescription from a doctor.

The dried leaves and flowers of the cannabis plant, Cannabis sativa, have been smoked or chewed for their narcotic effect for centuries.

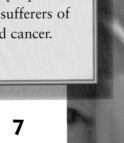

LEGALIZING CANNABIS

Cannabis (marijuana) is illegal in many countries, but pressure is increasing to legalize it for medicinal purposes. Smoking cannabis is said to bring great relief to sufferers of conditions like multiple sclerosis, arthritis, and cancer.

ALCOHOL

WHAT IS ALCOHOL?

You can make alcohol from almost anything edible. Through a process called fermentation, sugars are converted into ethanol alcohol. This chemical is readily absorbed into the bloodstream and has a powerful effect on the body and mind. Stronger alcohols, called spirits, and often called hard liquor, are made through distillation, in which alcohol is heated to concentrate the ethanol.

Different societies use different ingredients and processes to make alcohol. In southern Europe, grapes are traditionally fermented to make wine—a process first introduced by the Romans. Northern European countries are famous for their beers brewed from grain and hops. Grapes are also the main ingredient of another famous French spirit called brandy. Other spirits include gin, vodka, and whisky.

In countries such as Italy and France, wine-making is a huge industry. People enjoy wine with their meals and when they are relaxing.

TYPES OF ALCOHOL

Today there are many different kinds of alcohol, all with varying strengths and tastes. Wine comes in many forms from fizzy champagnes to red Bordeaux. Beers can vary from pale German lagers to dark Irish stouts. By mixing different drinks, such as brandy and wine, you can produce other alcohols like sherry. Sometimes spirits are flavored and sweetened to produce liqueurs like orange-flavored Cointreau or aniseed-flavored Pernod.

ALCOHOL STRENGTH

The strength of an alcoholic drink is known as its proof. Many producers put a percentage figure on the can or bottle that refers to the proof level, i.e., how much alcohol it contains. The higher the number, the less you can drink before the alcohol affects you.

During the brewing process, malt and other ingredients are mixed together, boiled, and fermented.

WINE COOLERS

Recently brewers have started putting small amounts of alcohol into fruit-flavored drinks, known as "wine coolers." They have been heavily criticized for deliberately appealing to younger people.

ATTITUDES TOWARD ALCOHOL

Although alcohol is a drug, it doesn't generally have the bad reputation that other drugs have. Many countries see it as an important part of their culture; in France, for instance, enjoying fine wines has been a sign of education and good taste for hundreds of years. Other countries, however, have in the past tried to ban alcohol. In America the Prohibition law banned alcohol for 13 years in the 1920s and 30s in an attempt to cut high drinking rates and resulting crime, poverty, and violence.

HOW STRONG IS THAT DRINK?

NAME	TYPE OF DRINK	ALCOHOL CONTENT
Wine cooler	Fruity drink with alcohol added	4%–8%
Beer	Fermented mixture of grains and water	3%–10%
Wine	Fermented grape juice	8%–14%
Liqueurs	Sweetened and flavored spirits	20%–40%
Spirits	Alcoholic drink concentrated by distillation	38%–45%

HOW DOES ALCOHOL AFFECT THE BODY?

Although it comes in different forms and strengths, alcohol has basically the same effects when you drink it. At first these may be pleasant. You may feel rather warm, light-headed, and relaxed.

However, the more you drink, the worse you will feel. As more alcohol enters your bloodstream, you will find it increasingly difficult to perform physical tasks.

You will lose your coordination and sense of balance, knocking things over and feeling unsteady on your feet. Your speech will become slurred and difficult for other people to understand.

One of the most common symptoms of having drunk too much is the sensation that the room is spinning. This comes with a sick feeling in the stomach and usually means that the person is going to vomit.

ALCOHOL IN THE BLOOD

When alcohol enters your stomach, it is quickly absorbed into the blood. It travels quickly up to the brain, where it interferes with brain function. This is what leads to so many physical and mental symptoms.

THE EFFECTS OF ALCOHOL

Being very drunk is highly unpleasant, both for you and those around you. You will probably vomit, and may lose control of your bladder. Eventually you will collapse and fall asleep until your body has been able to process some of the alcohol.

DANGERS OF ALCOHOL

If you drink a lot very quickly, alcohol can kill. It can affect the brain so badly that the heart or breathing stops. You also run the risk of choking if you vomit. Every night, hospitals treat people who have drunk too much.

People who have drunk far too much can get alcohol poisoning. In cases like this, hospitals have to pump the person's stomach to remove the alcohol.

BLOOD ALCOHOL LEVELS

The amount of alcohol you have drunk can be measured in milligrams (mg) of alcohol per 100 milliliters (ml) of blood. The measurement is related to how you feel and react. The effects also depend on your sex, size, age, how much you have eaten, and how used you are to drinking.

BLOOD ALCOHOL (mg/100 ml)	EFFECT ON A MODERATE DRINKER
20	Usually feel relaxed and able to "let go" slightly
60	Unable to make sensible decisions
100	Tend to be clumsy and unable to walk straight
180	Very drunk and unmanageable; later may not be able to remember what has happened
300	Often spontaneously incontinent. Possibly in coma.
500	Likely to die without medical help.

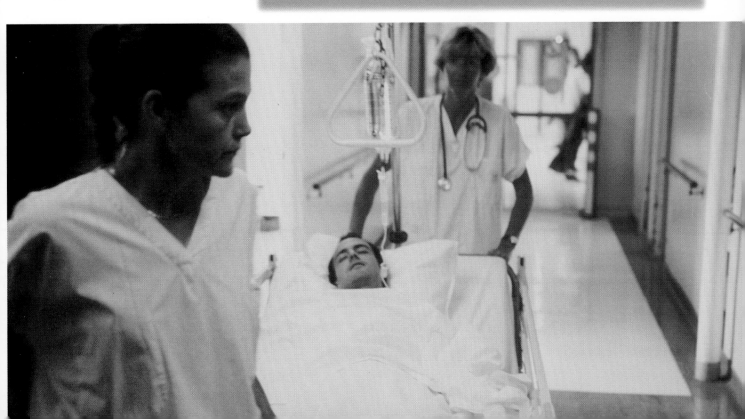

HOW ALCOHOL AFFECTS THE MIND

Alcohol also has powerful effects on the mind, altering your mood and the way you react. At first, you may feel more sociable, happy, and confident. This is one reason people like to drink, especially when they're socializing.

People who drink too much regularly can become an embarrassment to their friends because of their unpredictable and drunken behavior.

The more you drink, however, the worse you will feel. Alcohol is a depressant, and can make you feel more anxious or sad than normal. It affects your judgment, making you more likely to take risks. You can become paranoid and aggressive, misinterpreting what those around you say and do. Eventually you may be unable to recognize people, or even remember things like your own phone number. Alcohol can affect you so much that you may do things you would not normally consider.

This can have tragic consequences. Many unwanted pregnancies, crimes, suicides, and murders occur when someone is drunk.

WHAT'S IN THAT DRINK?

A 5-ounce glass of wine, a 12-ounce can of beer, and a 1.5 ounce shot of hard liquor contain roughly the same amount of alcohol. The American Medical Association refers to each of these as one "unit" of alcohol.

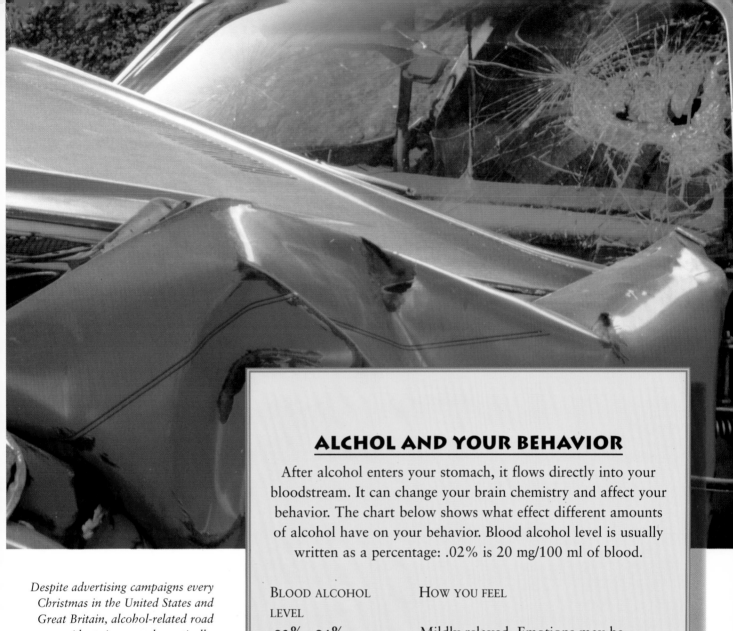

Despite advertising campaigns every Christmas in the United States and Great Britain, alcohol-related road accidents increase dramatically. People take risks driving when they are over the legal alcohol limit.

MEMORY LOSS

Most mental effects quickly reverse once the alcohol has left your body. However, your memory may be permanently damaged. People who get very drunk often wake up the next morning unable to remember what they did the night before.

ALCHOL AND YOUR BEHAVIOR

After alcohol enters your stomach, it flows directly into your bloodstream. It can change your brain chemistry and affect your behavior. The chart below shows what effect different amounts of alcohol have on your behavior. Blood alcohol level is usually written as a percentage: .02% is 20 mg/100 ml of blood.

BLOOD ALCOHOL LEVEL	HOW YOU FEEL
.02%–.04%	Mildly relaxed. Emotions may be slightly intensified
.05%–.07%	Warm and relaxed. Inhibitions are lost. Behavior may become exaggerated.
.08% and above	Judgment is affected. Motor skills are impaired and speech is slurred.

The present legal limit for blood alcohol while driving in the United States is .10%.

Many work days are lost due to hangovers. Often people describe having a hangover as feeling as if they've been poisoned.

DRINKING TOO MUCH

You may have heard adults complain about hangovers. Although they may joke about it, drinking too much can make people feel very sick the next day, and it can take days for their bodies to recover.

WHAT IS A HANGOVER?

Various things cause hangovers. Alcohol moves water out of body cells, leading to dehydration, which causes headaches. It upsets the stomach, making people feel sick. It destroys vital vitamins and lowers blood sugar, which is why hangovers often make people feel hungry. Alcohol also strains the liver and keeps you from sleeping well, which leaves you feeling exhausted and depressed. Generally a hangover feels like having been poisoned, which is exactly the case.

DOES EVERYONE SUFFER FROM HANGOVERS?

How bad someone feels depends mainly on how much they drink, although most people find that hangovers get worse as they grow older. Many adults try to avoid a

The liver is in the abdomen, below the diaphragm, and is attached to the stomach. It helps to digest and absorb fats and deals with the products of digestion. It also removes the poisons from substances like drugs and alcohol.

Blood from the intestines enters through the portal vein, and oxygenated blood from the heart enters via the hepatic artery. After being processed, blood leaves the liver through the hepatic vein, and waste products drain through the bile duct to the gall bladder.

ALCOHOL AND YOUR LIVER

The liver is the organ in your body that breaks down and eliminates poisons like alcohol. It has been likened to a car with one gear that just goes at one speed—the liver can burn up only one unit of alcohol an hour. Liver cells that have too much alcohol to process die and are replaced by fatty tissue.

Hepatic vein

Diaphragm

Gall bladder

Bile duct

Portal vein

Hepatic artery

hangover by not mixing different types of drinks, eating well beforehand or while drinking, and drinking plenty of non-alcoholic fluids to counteract dehydration.

IS THERE A CURE?

There are many reputed cures for hangovers, but time, rest, plenty of fluids, and healthy food are the best ways to help the body recover. Painkillers like aspirin may also relieve headaches, and antacids settle a queasy stomach. Of course, the best way to avoid a hangover is not to drink in the first place.

DID YOU KNOW?

Each year alcohol misuse leads to:
★ In the U.S.: $25 billion in alcohol-related injuries and illness.
   Over 40% of work accidents.
★ In Great Britain: 8–14 million lost working days.
   At least $90 million in related crime costs.
   Over $260 million a year in health expenditure.

LONG-TERM EFFECTS OF ALCOHOL

Although alcohol can make you feel bad the next day, drinking too much over a long period can make you very sick indeed. Drinking heavily over a number of years puts great strain on the liver, which can become so scarred that it no longer works properly. This is known as cirrhosis. Alcohol can also contribute to liver cancer.

ALCOHOL-RELATED DISEASES

Heavy drinking also contributes to other conditions like heart disease, hepatitis, and stomach problems such as bleeding and ulcers. It can cause men to become sexually impotent (see glossary), and by interfering with the balance of hormones in the body alcohol increases the risk of breast cancer in women. Mothers who drink heavily when pregnant can severely damage their unborn children; in the United States many babies are born with various deformities known as fetal alcohol syndrome.

This picture shows a damaged liver. Cirrhosis is a disease—often caused by heavy alcohol consumption—in which scars break up the structure of the liver. The symptoms of cirrhosis of the liver are vomiting blood, mental confusion, and jaundice.

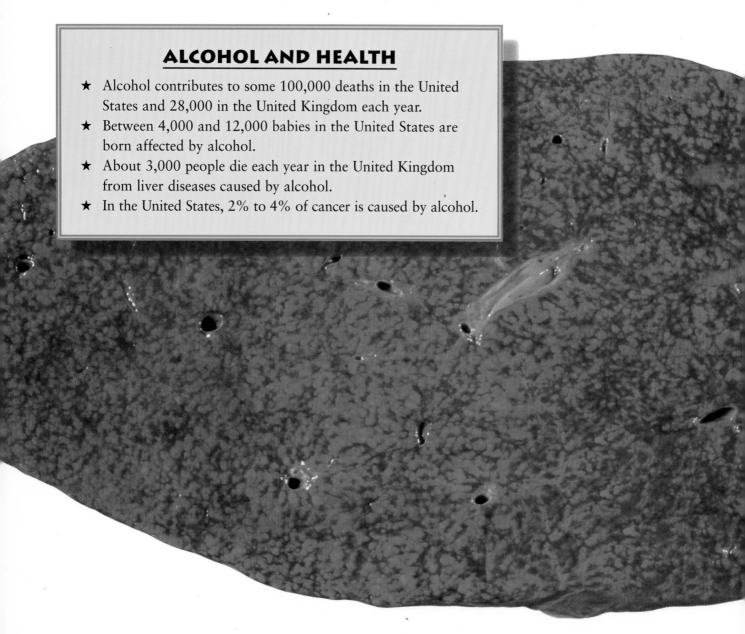

ALCOHOL AND HEALTH

★ Alcohol contributes to some 100,000 deaths in the United States and 28,000 in the United Kingdom each year.

★ Between 4,000 and 12,000 babies in the United States are born affected by alcohol.

★ About 3,000 people die each year in the United Kingdom from liver diseases caused by alcohol.

★ In the United States, 2% to 4% of cancer is caused by alcohol.

ALCOHOL AND WEIGHT GAIN

Alcohol is also very fattening. It is loaded with calories, which go directly into your bloodstream. A pint of beer, for instance, contains180 calories, as much as an average chocolate bar. Heavy drinkers can develop malnutrition,

People often forget to include their alcohol intake when they are counting calories. Just a few glasses of wine or a couple of beers can be as calorific as an entire meal.

because they get all their energy from alcohol instead of food, and alcohol lacks essential vitamins and minerals.

WOMEN AND ALCOHOL

Women are affected more seriously by a given amount of alcohol than men. This is partly because they are smaller, which concentrates the alcohol in their blood. Women also store more fat than men, and since alcohol can't dissolve in fat, it remains more active in their bodies.

DID YOU KNOW?

★ In the United States, more than 13 million adults have a drinking problem.

★ In the United States, nearly 2 million people over 12 receive treatment for alcohol problems.

★ In the United Kingdom about 35,000 people under 16 years old drink above the safe weekly limits for adults.

★ The United Kingdom has nearly 3 million problem drinkers —men who drink over 50 and women more than 35 units a week.

People may drink to forget the stresses and strains of modern living or to keep up with their friends. But dealing with constant hangovers takes the joy out of life and wastes time.

WHAT IS ALCOHOLISM?

People who drink heavily for a long time can become addicted to alcohol. Those who develop an emotional or physical dependency on drink are known as alcoholics. No one is exactly sure why they become dependent. It could be a genetic tendency; alcoholism sometimes runs in families. It may be that heavy drinkers have psychological problems or other problems from which drinking provides a temporary escape. Some experts, however, see alcoholism as a kind of disease.

ALCOHOL DEPENDENCY

Alcoholics, also known as problem or dependent drinkers, face more than just health problems. They may be unable to work effectively and can even lose their jobs. Drinking heavily inevitably affects their relationships with their families. Alcoholics may develop money problems or get into trouble with the police. They may then drink more heavily to get away from these problems.

GIVING UP ALCOHOL

Treatment programs for alcohol addiction can be very effective. Some people go to "drying out" clinics for help; others join groups like Alcoholics Anonymous for support in giving up alcohol. Alcoholics Anonymous has over two million members throughout the world.

SIGNS OF ALCOHOLISM

Alcoholism usually takes years to develop. Early signs include constantly needing to have liquor available and being unusually resistant to its effects. In the later stages, however, people gradually lose control over their drinking. They may need to have a drink as soon as they get up in the morning. Once they start drinking, they may well carry on until they are very drunk, which is known as binge drinking. Alcoholics often suffer from unpleasant conditions like shaking, various body pains, and redness in the face. They can experience severe withdrawal effects if they suddenly stop. Unlike coming off other drugs, sudden alcohol withdrawal can actually kill.

Being an alcoholic can be very lonely. The desire for alcohol becomes overpowering, and friendships and family are often neglected in favor of finding the next drink.

SMOKING

WHAT IS IN A CIGARETTE?

Cigarettes are made mainly from tobacco, the dried leaf of the plant *Nicotiana Tabacum*. Tobacco originated in Central America. There is evidence of smoking in the Mayan civilization there as long ago as A.D. 500. About 600 cigarette additives have been identified in American tobacco industry documents. Many of them are secret ingredients designed to give each brand a distinctive flavor.

Today tobacco-growing is one of the largest industries in the world.

Recently tobacco companies have been accused of deliberately adding flavors like cocoa, vanilla, and licorice to cigarettes to attract young smokers. There is no obligation for cigarette manufacturers to describe these additives on the pack.

CHEMICALS IN TOBACCO

The main components of cigarettes include nicotine, a powerful drug that quickly leads to addiction. Carbon monoxide, the same gas that comes out of car exhausts, is the principal gas in cigarette smoke. Other chemicals include many that have links with cancer in humans, such as arsenic, benzene, cadmium, and formaldehyde.

THE COST OF CIGARETTES

Cigarettes are expensive, particularly in states where taxation on tobacco is high. A pack of cigarettes costs nearly four dollars in many places. Smoking a pack a day over 20 years will cost nearly $30,000—assuming that prices don't rise further. That is enough to buy a new car.

The packing machine at the end of the manufacturing line fills countless packs of cigarettes for the world market.

WHAT HAPPENS WHEN I SMOKE?

When you take a puff on a cigarette, many things happen. In just a few seconds, nicotine is delivered to the brain. This stimulates the body's central nervous system, increasing the heart rate and blood pressure. Smoking also reduces the appetite and lowers skin temperature.

SMOKING RATES WORLDWIDE

COUNTRY	NUMBERS OF SMOKERS
China	300,000,000
United States	50,000,000
United Kingdom	12,000,000
Canada	6,000,000
Australia	3,500,000

CARBON MONOXIDE

Carbon monoxide gas, found in high concentrations in cigarette smoke, combines readily with hemoglobin, the substance in the blood that carries oxygen around the body.

Most smokers say that at certain times of the day, such as after a meal, they always crave a cigarette. Breaking these habits is the key to quitting smoking.

PREGNANCY AND TOBACCO

Pregnant women who smoke are putting the baby's health at serious risk. The baby is more likely to be born prematurely, or to die in the uterus (womb) or shortly after birth. Babies born to smokers are often smaller. They get less oxygen in the womb, which makes their hearts beat faster and slows their growth.

In heavy smokers, up to 15 percent of their blood can carry carbon monoxide instead of oxygen, depriving tissues and body cells of the oxygen they need to function. Long-term shortage of oxygen can cause problems with the growth, repair, and exchange of essential nutrients, increasing the risk of diseases like cancer.

If you are not used to smoking, you may notice other effects. Just one cigarette can make you feel sick and dizzy and may even make you vomit. These effects tend to wear off if you start smoking regularly.

Smoking—especially for pregnant women—is becoming less and less acceptable in the community. Laws have been passed in many of the states in the United States to prevent smoking in public places.

WHY IS SMOKING SO BAD FOR HEALTH?

Everyone knows that smoking is bad for your health, but not necessarily why. Smoking attacks your health in many ways. Carbon monoxide affects the electrical activity of the heart, encouraging fatty deposits to form on the artery walls. This increases the risk of heart attacks and other heart problems.

Smoking also raises the heart rate and blood pressure, which also increases the risk of heart attacks and bleeding in the brain, called strokes.

These are just some of the diseases that are more common in smokers than in nonsmokers.

Stroke
Blood loss to the brain. Often fatal or severely disabling.

Tobacco amblyopia
Defective vision.

Chronic bronchitis
Inflammation of the bronchial tubes leading into the lungs, resulting in coughing, wheezing, and fever.

Mouth and throat cancer

Lung cancer

Aortic aneurysm
A swelling of the main artery in the body, with the risk of rupture and fatal blood loss.

Emphysema
An often fatal lung disease, which destroys the walls of the air sacs.

Heart attack

Peptic ulcers
Raw and painful areas in the intestines.

Cancer of the cervix
(in women)

Lowered fertility

Gangrene
Death and decay of part of the body due to loss of blood supply when fatty deposits, caused by smoking, clog up the arteries.

Peripheral vascular disease
Disease of the arteries in the leg.

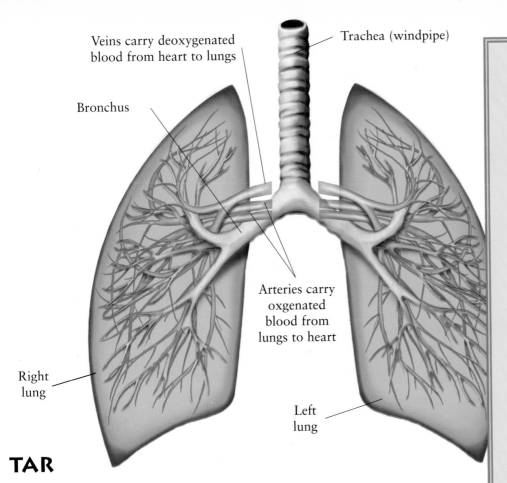

Veins carry deoxygenated blood from heart to lungs

Trachea (windpipe)

Bronchus

Arteries carry oxgenated blood from lungs to heart

Right lung

Left lung

TAR

Tar, one of the main byproducts of smoking even in low-tar brands, is also a killer. About 70 percent of the tar in inhaled cigarette smoke is deposited in the lungs, clogging them up and leading to coughs and breathlessness. Irritants in the tar also damage the delicate tissues of the lungs, increasing the risk of infection. Many of the chemicals present in tar are known to cause cancer, particularly lung cancer.

DEATH RATES

Every year 500,000 people in the United States and 120,000 in the UK die from smoking-related disease. Even when smoking doesn't lead to serious illness, it causes everyday complaints like coughing, bad breath, and shortness of breath.

Above The lungs put oxygen into the blood and remove toxic carbon dioxide from it. Smoking leaves tar deposits on the lungs, damaging them and making them less effective.

PASSIVE SMOKING

For most people, breathing in other people's cigarette smoke causes minor symptoms like watering eyes, itching nose and throat, and dizziness. But for some the effects are more serious. Babies and young children may suffer from more infections and serious chest conditions like bronchitis and pneumonia. People exposed to passive smoking over long periods are also at a 10 to 30 percent increased risk of death from lung cancer.

This is a smoker's lung. It is darker and rougher than a nonsmoker's lung and mis-shapen. Smoking inflames the lungs and scars them. It can also cause lung cancer.

25

WHY DO PEOPLE BECOME ADDICTED?

Smoking is very addictive. You have a 90 percent chance of getting hooked from smoking just a few cigarettes. This is mainly due to nicotine, which quickly produces effects on the brain when smokers are deprived of it. Smokers say that cigarettes make them feel more relaxed when they are tense, or more able to concentrate when they are tired, but much of this tenseness or tiredness is actually due to nicotine withdrawal.

SOCIAL PRESSURES TO SMOKE

This cycle of smoking and withdrawal can lead to chain-smoking, with heavy smokers getting through 40 to 60 cigarettes a day. But nicotine is not the only culprit. Young people often feel pressured into smoking by friends or acquaintances. You may start off smoking just to feel included, but quickly end up addicted. Cigarette advertising, banned in many countries, also encourages people to associate smoking with being cool or successful.

Many people find the smoke from other people's cigarettes irritating and unpleasant.

Smokers often say they find smoking comforting, especially in times of stress or upset. Many people enjoy the ritual of lighting up over a coffee or after a meal. This is what we call psychological addiction. Giving up these habits can be as difficult as coping with the physical craving.

MYTHS ABOUT SMOKING

Many people, girls in particular, start smoking to keep their weight down. Recent research, however, suggests that smoking in the longer term actually makes you fatter.

STARTING YOUNG

The first cigarettes smoked can feel and taste very unpleasant, yet many people start smoking in their teens. This is often because they feel that it makes them look older or "cool." Often people start simply because all their friends do. If someone comes from a smoking family, he or she may feel it is a natural part of growing up.

DID YOU KNOW?

★ In the United States, more than 3,000 young people under 18 years of age take up smoking every day. At least 4.5 million people under 18 smoke.

★ In the UK, 450 children under 16 start smoking each day; each year 11- to 15-year-olds smoke over 1 billion cigarettes. Almost one fourth of 15-year-olds are regular smokers.

People may choose to smoke because they believe it makes them look grown-up or sophisticated. Very often these people become addicted to tobacco and then are unable to quit smoking when they want to.

WHAT HAPPENS WHEN YOU TRY TO STOP?

All smokers know they would be better off if they gave up. Unfortunately, kicking the habit is not easy. Nicotine is as addictive as heroin, and it takes a lot of willpower to overcome the physical and psychological cravings. On average, seven out of ten smokers try and fail to quit at least twice. Sometimes people stop for years, only to light up again in a stressful situation.

WITHDRAWAL SYMPTOMS

That said, some 40 million U.S. smokers and 11 million UK smokers have quit. Most find that the first few days are the hardest, since nicotine withdrawal causes unpleasant symptoms such as lack of concentration, lightheadedness, anxiety, coughing, hunger, and strong cravings. These usually pass within a week or so.

Most smokers would like to give up smoking, but the stresses and strains of life make it hard for them to do so.

A HELPING HAND

There are many products and services available to help you quit smoking. These range from nicotine patches, gum, and lozenges, which lessen the physical craving by giving the body small amounts of the drug, to psychological aids, such as hypnotism, to reduce the urge to smoke.

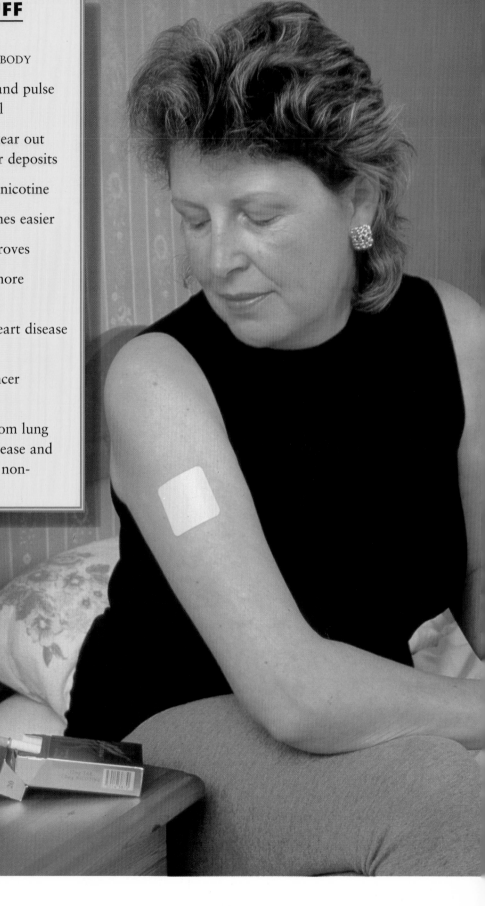

AFTER THE LAST PUFF

Time	Effects on the body
20 minutes later	Blood pressure and pulse return to normal
One day later	Lungs start to clear out mucus and other deposits
Two days later	Body is clear of nicotine
Three days later	Breathing becomes easier
2–12 weeks later	Circulation improves
3–9 months later	Lungs become more efficient
1 year later	Excess risk of heart disease is halved
10 years later	Risk of lung cancer reduced by half
15 years later	Risk of death from lung cancer, heart disease and stroke return to non-smoking levels.

QUITTING

Breaking the psychological dependency on smoking is just as difficult. People often have to change their routines and avoid places they associate with smoking. Being with other smokers is particularly hard when you are trying to quit. Within several months, however, most people find that even the urge to smoke disappears. Many even start to find smoking unpleasant.

The nicotine patch is just one of the many different methods of quitting that are available to smokers.

ILLEGAL DRUGS

WHAT HAPPENS WHEN YOU TAKE AN ILLEGAL DRUG?

People take illegal drugs for many reasons—because their friends do, for fun, to escape from their problems, or simply out of curiosity. But most people have no idea how these drugs act on their bodies or minds. Drugs act in different ways. Stimulants, such as cocaine, ecstasy, and speed, act on your body's central nervous system and increase brain activity. Depressants, like alcohol, solvents, and sedatives, also affect the central nervous system, but actually slow down brain activity.

Hallucinogens, like cannabis, LSD, and magic mushrooms, influence the mind, distorting the way you see and hear things. Exactly how a drug affects you depends on many things—like your size, whether you have taken anything else like alcohol, and how used you are to that particular drug. It also depends on how you take it.

TYPES OF ILLEGAL DRUGS

DRUG	STREET NAMES	USUAL FORM	HOW TAKEN
Amphetamine	Speed, uppers	Powder or tablets	Swallowed, sniffed
Cannabis	Marijuana, dope, ganja, grass, hash, weed	Leaf form (grass); brown/black resin (hash or hashish)	Smoked or eaten
Cocaine	Coke, blow, snow, crack	White powder, crystals	Sniffed or smoked
Ecstasy	E, XTC, doves	Pills	Swallowed
Heroin	Smack, horse, junk	Brown or white powder	Injected, sniffed, or smoked
LSD	LSD, acid	Tablets, impregnated paper	Swallowed
Magic mushrooms	'Shrooms	Dried/fresh mushrooms (psilocybin)	Eaten
Sedatives	Barbiturates, Temazepam	Tablets	Swallowed
Solvents		Glue, lighter fuel, nail polish, gasoline, aerosols	Inhaled

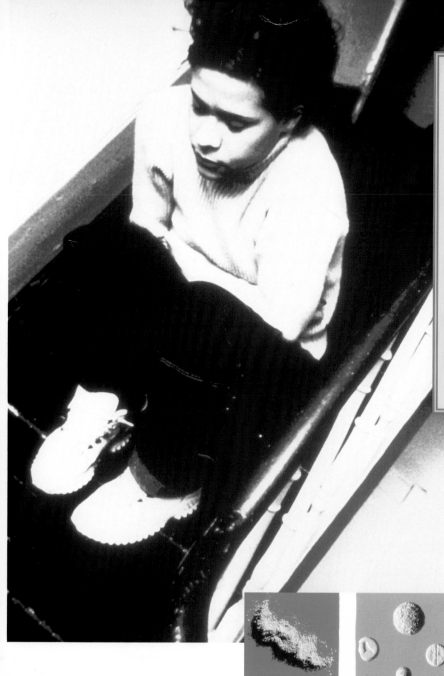

There are normally few physical signs that someone has taken an illegal drug. Although drugs often cause the pupils of the eyes to dilate, usually the only sign will be a change in behavior. With heroin or cannabis, someone may seem more dopey and quiet than usual; with amphetamines, cocaine, or ecstasy, they may appear more lively.

It is impossible to tell whether the drug you are buying has been properly manufactured or not. A bad reaction can produce frightening symptoms in people.

Injecting or snorting a drug tends to have a faster and more powerful effect than swallowing one.

KNOWING WHAT YOU'RE GETTING

Another problem with illegal drugs is that you can never be sure exactly what is in them. Many cases of overdose or harm occur because a drug is too pure or is contaminated with other substances.

From left to right, pictured are nine illegal drugs: heroin, esctasy, cannabis (grass), magic mushroom, LSD, cannabis resin (hash), cocaine, crack, and speed.

HOW DO DRUGS MAKE YOU FEEL?

Many people drink alcohol because they like the taste, but most people take illegal drugs to make them feel different. These feelings depend on the drug. While ecstasy produces feelings of friendliness and happiness, cannabis can make things seem funnier than usual, and it heightens enjoyment of food and music.

BAD REACTIONS

However, most illegal drugs can make you feel very bad indeed. You never know how you will react to an illegal or abused substance. You may feel fine, for instance, the first dozen times you take cannabis, then suddenly experience strong feelings of fear or paranoia. LSD and mushrooms in particular can produce "bad trips"—extreme feelings of anxiety, fear, paranoia, even nightmare visions.

WHO TAKES DRUGS?

In the United States, drug use is highest in people from ages 18 to 25. In the population overall, about a third of people have taken drugs at some point in their life. For those aged 18 to 25, as many as 25 percent have taken drugs within the last year.

Unfortunately, if you do have a bad reaction, all you can do is wait for the effects to wear off.

MOOD

A lot depends on the mood you are in when you take a drug. Cannabis heightens whatever you are feeling at the time, so if you are more anxious or depressed than usual, the drug can make you feel worse. As with alcohol, drugs

Above Paranoia is a common reaction to certain drugs. The user becomes afraid and thinks that he or she is being persecuted or chased.

Right In many nightclubs, owners are trying to prevent the use of ecstasy.

also affect your reactions. You will find it more difficult to control how you feel and what you do if something happens to you.

DRUGS AND THEIR EFFECTS

Drug	Good feelings	Bad feelings	How long it lasts
Amphetamines	Wakefulness, happiness	Anxiety, panic	3–4 hours
Cannabis (Marijuana)	Relaxation, relief from boredom, enhancement of sensory awareness	Paranoia, panic	1–12 hours
Cocaine and crack cocaine	Exhilaration, well-being, indifference to pain or tiredness	Insomnia, "crash" (bad mood—result of withdrawal)	20–30 minutes. Crack lasts 10–12 minutes.
Ecstasy	Happiness, friendliness, energy, calmness	Nausea, fatigue, and depression after use	Several hours
Heroin	Happiness, contentment, warmth, peacefulness	Nausea, vomiting	3–4 hours, depending on how taken
LSD/ muschrooms	Fascinating sounds and visual hallucinations, euphoria	Waking nightmares, paranoia	12 hours
Sedatives	Calmness, relaxation	Nausea, vomiting	Several hours
Solvents	Hallucinations, euphoria	Hangovers, drowsiness	Few minutes

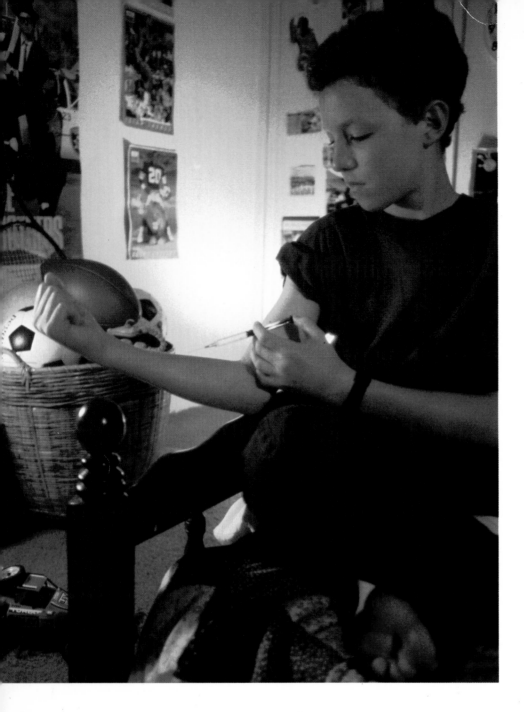

This boy is using a syringe to inject himself with drugs. Because there are very few physical symptoms, parents may not find out that their child is using drugs until he or she has become addicted.

METHADONE

Most Western countries have programs to help people fight heroin and other drug addictions. Methadone can help some people addicted to heroin come off the drug without feeling all the withdrawal symptoms. There are also residential centers where addicts can try to give up within a safe and supportive environment, and there are alternatives such as counseling, self-help groups, and educational activities.

WHY ARE SOME DRUGS ADDICTIVE?

Most illegal or abused substances are not addictive. If you use cannabis, ecstasy, amphetamines, LSD, or solvents, for example, you can't become addicted to them in the same way you might to cigarettes or even alcohol, because your body won't come to depend on them.

PHYSICAL DEPENDENCY

Unfortunately, this is not true of heroin, cocaine, crack, or sedatives. You can become physically dependent on these drugs, which means that you need them to feel well or normal, and you experience withdrawal symptoms if you suddenly stop taking them.

How quickly you become addicted depends on how much and how often you take the drugs, as well as on your personality and circumstances.

EXPERIMENTING WITH DRUGS

Many people experiment with heroin, for instance, without becoming addicted; it may take several weeks or months of heavy use to become dependent. Crack cocaine, however is rapidly addictive. Just because you are not physically addicted to a drug doesn't mean you're not dependent on it in other ways. If you feel you cannot enjoy yourself without smoking pot or taking ecstasy, then you have become psychologically dependent on the drug to function normally.

These vials contain white crack crystals. Crack comes from cocaine and is highly addictive and very strong. Crack users heat the crystals to produce a vapor, which they then inhale.

HEROIN/CRACK ADDICTION

★ At least 22 million U.S. citizens have tried cocaine; 1.7 million are regular users.

★ 4.6 million people in the U.S. have used crack, 1.3 million within the last year.

★ Nearly 3 million people in the U.S. have used heroin.

★ In the U. S., at least 600,000 people use heroin every year.

★ In 1996, there were 43,372 registered UK heroin addicts—about 20 to 30 percent of the total number of addicts.

★ Less than 1 percent of the UK population use heroin, and 2 percent use cocaine.

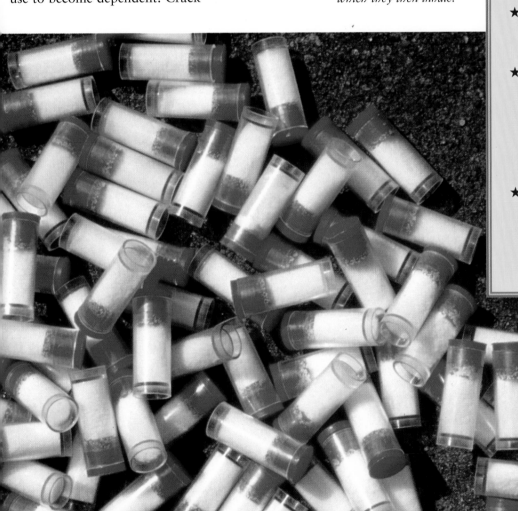

HOW DRUGS AFFECT PEOPLE IN THE LONG RUN

Once addicted to a drug, people will do anything to get their next fix—even break the law.

Even if most drugs don't lead to addiction, they can be habit forming. The temptation is to take them more and more frequently. You may have heard the saying "there's no such thing as a free lunch." This is particularly true of drugs. While no one would deny that taking them can make you feel good in the short term, over time they will take their toll on both your body and your mind.

DRUGS AND CRIME

★ Long-term drug use is extremely expensive. A lot of crimes are committed in order to pay for drugs like heroin and crack.

★ Heroin addicts need more than $19,000 a year to pay for heroin.

★ In 1996, nearly 16 percent of convicted prisoners said they had committed their offense to get money for drugs.

★ About 36 percent of convicted prisoners said they were using drugs at the time of their offense.

COMING DOWN

Some drugs like cocaine and ecstasy make you pay for the pleasure they give by leaving you feeling tired and depressed for several days afterward. Over long-term use, the physical effects of drugs can be greater.

Cocaine can cause heart problems, chest pain, and even convulsions and can permanently damage the lining of your nose. Ecstasy has been linked to liver and kidney problems. Long term use of amphetamines can put a strain on your heart. As with tobacco, smoking a lot of marijuana puts you at risk of throat and lung cancer.

PAYING THE PRICE

With many other drugs, however, the effects are more subtle. Smoking marijuana long term, for instance, often leads to a lack of motivation and feelings of apathy. It can also impair the ability to learn and concentrate, making it even harder to get on with life. One of the problems with illegal drugs is that they are not tested for safety in the same way as medical drugs. No one knows, therefore, what the long-term effects of a drug may be, particularly for newer substances like ecstasy.

A razor blade is used to chop up speed (an amphetamine) into a fine powder, which is then snorted.

DRUGS AND YOUR MENTAL HEALTH

Some drugs can permanently affect your mental health. LSD and magic mushrooms can lead to flashbacks, where you temporarily relive some aspect of your "trip," even years afterward. More worryingly, these hallucinogens can trigger severe mental health problems like depression and schizophrenia in vulnerable people. There is increasing evidence that ecstasy can permanently change the chemicals in your brain, making you more vulnerable to depression and anxiety.

CAN DRUGS REALLY KILL?

People used to think that all drugs were extremely dangerous and taking them inevitably led to addiction and death. Although this put a lot of people off drugs, many others discovered that this simply wasn't true.

Although many people use drugs recreationally without serious side-effects, for some it can end in tragedy.

DRUG DEATHS

The following table shows rough averages of drug deaths per year in the United States in the 1990s.

DRUG	DEATHS
Tobacco	400,000
Alcohol	100,000
Hard drugs	6,000

RISKS

However, taking any drug is always a gamble. You cannot tell what is in it or how you will react. Combining different drugs, especially on top of drinking alcohol, is particularly risky. The sad fact is that taking illegal drugs does kill a significant number of people every year.

One of the most dangerous drug activities is abusing solvents like glue or aerosols. The risk of suffocation or choking on vomit is high, as is the chance of sudden heart failure. Heroin and crack cocaine can kill through overdose, particularly if the drug is unexpectedly pure. Ecstasy has led to a significant number of deaths, because it encourages overheating and dehydration in users. Some users have died from drinking too much water to compensate.

DRUG-RELATED DEATHS

Not all deaths are related directly to the drug. Like alcohol, many illegal drugs kill by increasing the risk of accidents. Driving under the effect of illegal drugs is particularly foolish, and may harm others as well as yourself.

Becoming dependent on drugs can have other consequences. Drugs are very expensive and buying them can lead to financial problems. You can also lose your friends or even your job if the effects of taking drugs start to alter your behavior or your ability to function normally.

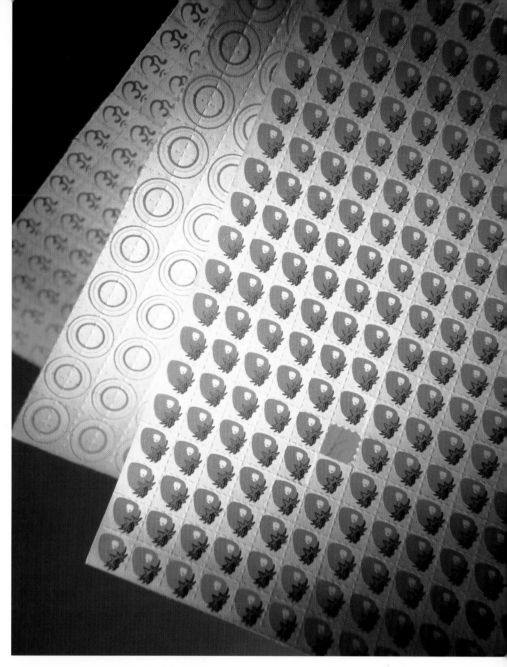

LSD is made in the form of pills and as sheets of blotting paper that are cut into squares and impregnated with the drug.

LSD, or "acid," is illegal in most countries but is widely used as a recreational drug.

HALLUCINATIONS

Some drugs like LSD, magic mushrooms, or even cannabis can cause hallucinations: you see, hear, or feel things that aren't really happening. Hallucinations can be very frightening. Many drugs cause panic attacks, which can be very alarming, even leading people to believe that they are dying. This is particularly likely if someone is anxious or worried about the drug's effects.

MEDICINAL DRUGS

HOW DO MEDICINAL DRUGS AFFECT ME?

Not so long ago, the only drugs or medicines available for people were substances extracted from plants and sometimes animals. Indeed, in some countries, like China, the use of herbs and other plants is still a popular way of treating the sick.

Despite dramatic leaps in medical technology, some illnesses, such as the common cold and flu, still have no cure.

THE PLACEBO EFFECT

New drugs are always tested to make sure they are safe and effective, by giving the drug to one group and a pretend version to another. An interesting discovery arising from these tests is that even those people given the dummy version often find that their symptoms improve. This has come to be known as the "placebo effect" and is proof that the mind can have a great influence on the course of disease in our bodies.

Antibiotics are used to treat bacterial infections and to protect people with weak immune systems. Some antibiotics treat only certain types of bacteria while others deal with a wide range of bacteria.

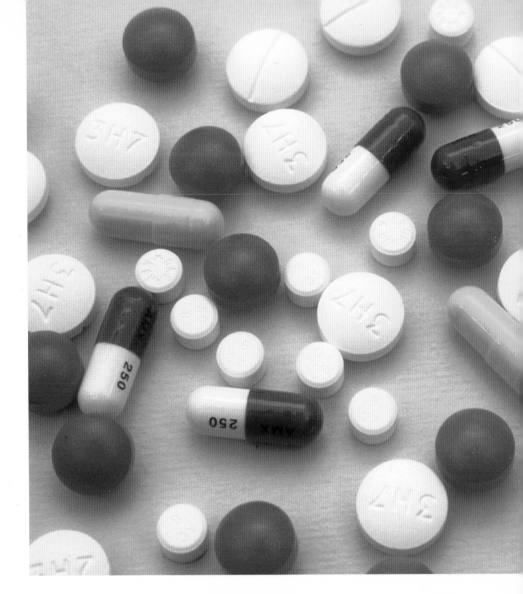

DEVELOPING DRUGS

In much of the world, however, modern medicine relies heavily on drugs created in the laboratory, manufactured through various chemical processes. There are drugs for every type of illness and disorder, and thousands more are developed every year.

HOW DO THEY WORK?

While the exact workings of some drugs are poorly understood, most work by replacing deficient chemicals in the body, interfering with the ways in which cells function or combating infectious diseases and bacteria directly. Some drugs work very rapidly to relieve symptoms of disease; others can take months to have any effect.

SIDE EFFECTS

Even useful drugs can have unwanted effects on the body. These are called "side effects." When you take a drug, it travels to all parts of your body and may work on parts other than those affected by the illness or disease. Some people are more vulnerable to side effects than others, and may even stop taking a drug because of them.

COMMON DRUGS AND SIDE EFFECTS

Drug	Use	Side effects
Fluoxetine (Prozac)	Antidepressant	Headache, diarrhea, anxiety
Aspirin	Painkiller	Indigestion
Morphine	Painkiller	Drowsiness, nausea, constipation
Ranitidine (Zantac)	Anti-ulcer drug	Headache
Antibiotics	Anti-infection drug	Diarrhea, rash

DRUGS IN SPORTS

Drug	Why taken	Is it banned?	Why?
Anabolic steroids	To build muscle bulk	Yes	Gives users an unfair advantage and is associated with many health problems
Caffeine	To stimulate the body	Only in very large quantities	
Cocaine	To stimulate the body	Yes	Many health risks
Morphine	To reduce or relieve pain	Yes	Can cover up underlying fitness problems

ABUSING MEDICINAL DRUGS

Medicinal drugs can be just as powerful as illegal drugs like heroin or cocaine, and just as dangerous if not used properly. Sometimes medicinal drugs are deliberately abused; the sleeping pill Temazepam is sometimes sold on the street. Melting down these capsules and injecting them into the bloodstream can cause blockages, sometimes leading to limb amputations or even death.

ADVERSE REACTIONS

More often, however, medicinal drugs cause accidental harm. All drugs are chemicals, and can have a toxic effect on the body. Some people have an adverse reaction to a drug they need, and in extreme cases this can kill. Sometimes one drug may react with another that a person is taking, producing powerful and unwanted results.

MIXING DRUGS

Other drugs, such as alcohol, can interfere with certain medications like some antidepressants, sedatives, and antibiotics. Sometimes drugs like antihistamines, used to treat allergies, can make users very drowsy, and increase the chances of car wrecks or industrial accidents.

Anabolic steroids improve performance by stimulating muscle and bone growth.

DANGERS OF MEDICINAL DRUGS

Drugs can be dangerous in different situations. Young children should never take the painkiller aspirin as it can sometimes cause a potentially fatal condition called Reye's Syndrome. Pregnant women must avoid drugs that could damage the unborn baby. In the 1960s, for instance, many children were born handicapped because their mothers were prescribed the anti-nausea drug Thalidomide during pregnancy.

Sometimes people become addicted to medicinal drugs. For many years doctors prescribed tranquilizers to treat anxiety, not realizing that their patients were becoming addicted to them.

It is very important to follow the instructions precisely when taking medicinal drugs. Otherwise they may produce adverse reactions.

CANCER CURE

Occasionally the toxic effects of a drug are deliberate. The common cancer treatment chemotherapy works by poisoning the cells in the body. The hope is that the healthy ones will recover, while the cancerous cells die. Because of this toxicity, chemotherapy is often an unpleasant treatment to undergo.

BEING SENSIBLE

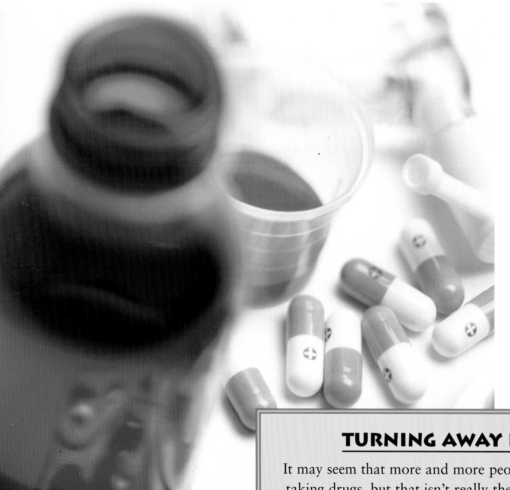

Few people would suggest that we ban alcohol completely. Indeed, many people depend on it for their jobs, and alcohols such as wine are appreciated by millions of people across the world without posing a great risk to their health. Also, small amounts of alcohol have been shown to actually lower the risk of heart disease.

AVOIDING THE RISKS

Other drugs, however, such as tobacco and illegal drugs, are always best avoided. No one will claim that taking them is likely to kill you—at least, not immediately.

TURNING AWAY FROM DRUGS

It may seem that more and more people are smoking, drinking, and taking drugs, but that isn't really the case. In the United States and Western Europe, drinking alcohol has actually decreased over the last 100 years. In the UK smoking has decreased from 50 percent of adults smoking in 1972 to around 30 percent today. Even fears that we are in the grip of an escalating drug crisis could be a popular myth; the largest UK survey of drug misuse shows that drug taking is not part of normal behavior for the vast majority of young people.

Nearly all drugs are potentially dangerous if taken irresponsibly— even cold and flu remedies.

But all of them are bad for your health in one way or another and can have serious consequences for you physically and mentally. Many of these consequences only show up later in life; unfortunately by then it is often too late to do anything about them.

LIFE-SAVING DRUGS

Medicines, on the other hand, save thousands of lives every year. We are lucky to be living at a time when we have chemicals to help cure and control the diseases that have plagued humankind for thousands of years. Antibiotics can cure infections that would have killed less than a century ago.

But all drugs, even medicines, have to be used sensibly. Too many antibiotics, for instance, can actually provoke disease, by encouraging the bacteria that cause disease to mutate. Those people who avoid harmful drugs and treat medicines with respect stand to gain the most from what these modern chemicals can offer.

With so many medicines available to us today, modern life has the potential to be full and active. To realize this potential, people must take a sensible approach to drugs and alcohol.

GLOSSARY

Amputation The cutting off of a limb for a medical reason.

Antacids Medicine taken for certain stomach upsets.

Apathy A feeling of not caring about anything.

Arteries The main blood-carrying tubes in your body.

Bacteria Tiny organisms that sometimes cause diseases.

Central nervous system The brain and the spinal cord system controlling the body's working and reactions.

Convulsion A violent series of muscle contractions.

Craving A desperate wish to have something.

Dehydration An abnormal loss of water from the body.

Depression A feeling of sadness over a period of time.

Dilate To widen or expand.

Drug dependence Inability to live and cope without taking a particular drug.

Fermentation A chemical reaction that breaks down a molecule, such as when yeast breaks down sugar into alcohol.

Genetic Inherited from parents.

Hallucinations Visions of something that isn't actually there.

Hepatitis A disease of the liver.

Incontinence An inability to control the bladder or bowels, often brought on by excessive alcohol intake.

Immune system The system that the body relies on to defend itself from infection.

Impregnate To saturate or soak an item with something, such as a liquid.

Inhale To breathe and draw air or other gases into the lungs.

Mineral A substance that is neither animal nor vegetable.

Muslim A person who believes and follows the Islamic religion.

Paranoia A feeling that people are "out to get you."

Persecution The act of hounding and mistreating someone.

Placebo Something, such as a drug, that is ineffective but is given to make people think that they are being treated.

Plantation An estate where huge crops, such as tobacco, rubber, and bananas, are grown for export to other countries.

Psychological Relating to the mind or feelings.

Schizophrenia A mental illness that results in people's withdrawing from society and hallucinating.

"Snort" To inhale something, such as a drug, through the nose.

Steroids Drugs, such as anabolic steroids, that can be used to improve performance in sports by building up muscle.

Stimulant Something that excites or speeds the workings of the mind or body.

UK United Kingdom of Great Britain and Northern Ireland. Great Britain is the island made up of England, Scotland, and Wales.

Ulcer A sore area on the inside or outside of your body.

Vapor When a liquid evaporates, it forms particles of moisture, which are called vapor.

Vial A small bottle used to contain liquids.

Vitamin An element that is essential in small quantities for providing nutrition to the body.

Withdrawal The period that a drug-user goes through after giving up using drugs. Usually associated with physical and mental side effects.

FURTHER INFORMATION

FURTHER READING

Barbour, Scott (ed.) *Alcohol!* (Opposing Viewpoints). San Diego, CA: Greenhaven Press, 1997.

Bayer, Linda N. *Amphetamines and Other Uppers* (Jr. Drug Awareness). Broomall, PA: Chelsea House, 1999.

Claypool, Jane. *Alcohol and You* (Impact). Danbury, CT: Franklin Watts, 1997.

Cohen, Daniel. "Prohibition: America Makes Alcohol Illegal." *Spotlight on American History*. Brookfield, CT: Millbrook Press, 1995.

Harris, Jacqueline. *Drugs and Disease* (Bodies in Crisis). New York: 21st Century Books, 1995.

Haughton, Emma. *A Right to Smoke* (Viewpoints). Danbury, CT: Franklin Watts, 1997.

Hyde, Margaret O. *Know About Smoking*. New York: Walker and Co., 1995.

Johnston, Marianne. *Let's Talk About Alcohol Abuse* (The Let's Talk About Library). New York: Rosen Publishing Group, 1997.

Lang, Alan R. "Alcohol: Teenage Drinking." *The Encyclopedia of Psychoactive Drugs*. New York: Chelsea House, 1992.

McGuire, Paula. *Alcohol* (Preteen Pressures). Austin, TX: Raintree Steck-Vaughn, 1998.

Pringle, Laurence. *Drinking: A Risky Business*. New York: William Morrow, 1997.

Robbins, Paul R. *Crack and Cocaine Drug Dangers* (Drug Dangers). Springfield, NJ: Enslow, 1999.

Ryan, Elizabeth A. *Straight Talk about Drugs and Alcohol* (Straight Talk). New York: Facts on File, 1995.

Seixas, Judith S. *Living with a Parent Who Drinks Too Much*. New York: William Morrow, 1983.

FINDING OUT MORE

Alcohol and Drug Problems Association of North America
1101 15th Street, NW
Suite 204
Washington, DC 20005

Alcoholics Anonymous
PO Box 459
Grand Central Station
New York, NY 10163
Tel: (212) 870 3400

MADD
(Mothers Against Drunk Driving)
511 E. John Carpenter Freeway
Irving, TX 75062

NCADD
(National Council on Alcoholism and Drug Dependence)
12 West 21st Street
New York, NY 10010
Tel: (212) 206 6770

WEBSITES

http://www.ncadd.org
American site with links to many other related sites.

http://www.alcoholconcern.org.uk
Home page for the UK organization Alcohol Concern.

http://www.nzdf.org
The New Zealand Drugs Foundation home page.

http://www.eurocare.org
A website with Europe-wide news, information, and discussions about alcohol.

INDEX

48